The Choice

By

Devanshu Vatsa

Bird Features & Writing Agency
New Delhi-110059

ISBN: 9798413856253

Publisher	:	Bird Features & Writing Agency, 404, F-52-53, Street no. 10 Om vihar extn. Uttam Nagar West New Delhi-110059.
Website	:	www.birdfeatures.in
E-mail	:	birdfeatures@gmail.com
First Edition	:	2022
Price	:	$ 8.99
Cover	:	Simpal Chaman
Type Setting	:	Chanda Singh

The Choice (Collection of short stories) By Devanshu Vatsa

Preface

How will be that time when we have to stay away from the world of modern science? Something similar happened with the Pyuricans! What happened after that... read this story...

Along with this, other stories of the author have been included in this book.

-Publisher

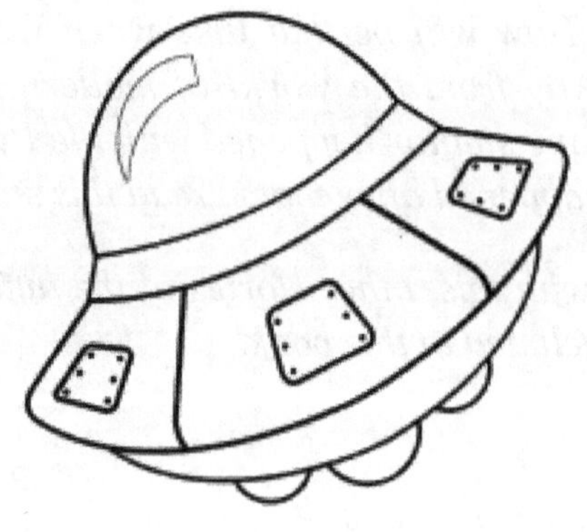

Science Fiction

The Choice

A long time had passed traveling in the spaceship and we had come very close to the Pyorican. As we were approaching that unknown planet, the brightness of Prof. Bhaskaran's face was increasing.

"This strange planet was discovered by my father. He was of native Negro race, but my mother was an Indian. My mother passed away when I was very young. To keep fresh her memory, Papa named this planet- Pyorican......"- Professor Told in his own tune.

"What was her name?" - I interrupted.

"Priyanka, but Papa used to call her by the name-'Pyari'." Then Professor Started studying that planet. It is about 6.5 light years away from our Earth.

Light travels 2,99,776 km in a second and there are about thirty five millions seconds in a year….. In this way we had come billions of kilometers away from the earth.

Now visuals of the planet were starting to emerge on the screen. Suddenly we were shocked. A strange sight was coming on the screen. The scene was of a field. Some children were playing. Unique children......... small arms and legs, weak body and a big distorted shaped head. The scene focused on a boy. Professor instructed the computer to study the child deeply. Suddenly the child started growing at an uncontrollable rate, then grew old, eventually died. We were shocked. Seeing this, it seemed as if a video film had been given a fast pace.

"Professor, I think the time has become irregular here. You remember, don't you... I gave you a book by J. G. Ballard to read - 'Memoirs of Space Age'. There is mention of being irregular of time. It seems, perhaps, there is such thing here too! "

".....Oh no. It's just a science fiction."- Professor Bhaskaran said cutting my point.

""But Professor, the science fiction of yesterday is the truth of today. Two-three hundred years ago, airplanes, computers, etc. were only imagined. Many science fictions have turned out to be true." I was telling but the professor's attention was not on my side.. He was busy doing a comparative study of that planet with the Earth. According to the data obtained from the computer, there were six other planets in this solar system besides this Pyurican. It was a little older than Earth. The amount of oxygen and nitrogen here was very less.

" Professor, So far we have made three rounds of this planet, but we have not got any signal. I think, Quasir has forgotten." - I expressed my doubts.

Quasir was a well-known scientist of the Pyurican.

"It may be. After a year of his calling, we have reached the Pyorican. The distance is so much what we can do." After stopping for some time, Professor Said, "I think Quasir……." Then the computer started to make a beep-beep sound. Some signals were coming on the screen. ...... Yes, this signal was from Quasir, which was allowing our spaceship to land.

Our spacecraft had landed on the Pyorican. The Pyorican, which looked green from afar, now looked frightening and desolate. There was flat land far and wide and the atmosphere was also very hot. In the sultry air, we were staring here and there.

"Welcome, our honored guests." Then a voice came. We looked here and there. There was nothing in the distance except our spacecraft. Again the same voice came, - "Sorry for the inconvenience caused to you. In no time you will be able to see everything."

Then slowly everything became clear. We were in front of a huge laboratory. We entered. The laboratory stretched for hundreds of meters. There was a cabin in front of us. Inside, Quasir, with small arms and legs, a weak body and a large skull, was so weak that he could only speak. When the cabin glass got invisible, we went inside.

"I have been like this for thousands of years." - said Quasir. We were surprised to hear this and remembered the old sages.

"What, the whole land here is like this..." - Prof. Bhaskaran asked in surprise and impatience.

"No, this is my laboratory. I have made this place to protect from external enemies. You cannot see anything here without my wish." - said Quasir.

"Why did your situation happen like this" - I asked seeing Quasir's condition.

"Let me tell you. Please you guys also sit down." - He gestured to sit down. He was trying to be normal. His breathing was off. But he was all right.

"I am one of the great scientists of this planet. There are other planets in our solar system. But there is no sign of life on them. Our science was progressing at a rapid pace. On the one hand our population is increasing rapidly. On the other hand, the vegetation was decreasing. Due to this the amount of oxygen on our planet has reduced considerably. But human is also a wonderful creature. He adapts himself to it even in the most difficult situations. We learned the photosynthesis from plants. This enabled us to live without oxygen. But other creatures proved unable to do so and eventually disappeared."

"Here every human was seeking knowledge and only knowledge. He started doing more and more mental exercises. All the rest of the work was done by computers and robots. We had evolved so much that computers were controlled by mental waves only. Any work could have been done just by our wish."

"But later we realized our mistake. Computers used to do all the work, big and small. Our body became weak due to lack of physical labor. Women were unable to give birth to children. Test tube babies began to be made in the laboratory. But we could not conquer death. On the other hand, test tube babies also proved incapable of fighting pollution. We had all the facilities but we started seeing our very existence in danger.

"To save our existence, we discovered an alternative. We established the contact of various waves emanating from the human brain with the supercomputer. As well other elements like genes, hormones, enzymes that control the essential functions of the body's life, we controlled those things with the help of computer. We had conquered old age and death.

"This was made possible only by an elaborate computer network. The task of controlling this task was entrusted to five other scientists along with me. But due to some technical glitch in the supercomputer, all five of them have died." - Quasir was speaking looking at the void.

"But how did all this happen....." - Prof. Bhaskaran asked, looking intently at the helpless Quasir.

“Let me tell...”- the weary Quasir paused and began to say again,- “The speed of time is also strange. For about ten thousand years we kept supercomputers under the control of our mental waves. But two years ago there was some technical fault in the super computer. Despite a lot of effort we were not able to control it. Now the situation is that everyone’s age here has become irregular, uncontrolled and erratic. Some live their whole life in a moment, while some are unable to spend even half a minute of their months of life.”- Saying this, Quasir became silent.

“You must have taken preventive measures”- I asked.

“Yes, I informed the planets of other solar systems. Scientists came from there, but seeing the situation here, they realized the irregularity of time and they went back on their feet. I had a feeling that you too would return. But you came. There is no place for my death also.” Sadness was clearly visible on Quasir’s face. He added, “Now you have to find the option to avoid this crisis.”

“We will try our best.”- we said, assuring Quasir.

With Quasir, we tried to find and fix supercomputer malfunctions for several days, but with no success. In fact, the science there was far ahead than on Earth. In the end we came to the conclusion that the entire computer network should be destroyed. Hearing this, the tired Quasir's face became even more sad and worried. Anyway, time and worry had made his face emotionless and radiant.

"As soon as the supercomputer network is destroyed, all our computers will be destroyed. Because we haven't set up a lifetime network separately. We will go back millions of years in terms of science. All our technical knowledge is in these computers. Even though we have done our physical development to a great extent in these days. Our fertility is also normal now. But we are again in a position to go back to the primeval period." - Quasir was in an ocean of despair.

We left the laboratory and headed towards the main computer chamber. It was eighty kilometers away from the city. We went there by hydrogen powered car. This was probably Quasir's last voyage in a computer-controlled car.

The view on the way was strange. A man was motionless in a moving state like an idol. He was unable to even think because of a computer problem. Only then a child started becoming an adult at an uncontrolled pace and on seeing it became old and died. Seeing everything, there was no sense of irregularity of time. Here everyone's life and death were uncertain and uncontrolled. If anyone was normal, it was just a coincidence.

In no time we were in the main computer chamber. On the instructions of Quasir, Prof. created a data. Quasir pressed Enter. A loud sound of beep..beep started coming from the computer. All of a sudden the computers stopped working. A scream mixed with joy and sorrow came out of Quasir's mouth. There was nothing left in the name of science on this planet named Pyurican. All the equipment was now just models.

The Pyoricans, who had enjoyed science for years, were in an instant, millions of years behind. But now all were far from uncontrolled and uncertain life and death. Quasir's car was also now worthless. Then many Pyuritans had also arrived. There was more joy on his face than the sadness of losing science. The clouds of sadness were now removed from Quasir's face.

"We could have done this before, but then our contact with the outside world would be cut off forever." - said Quasir.

We departed after accepting a request from the Pyorican to send a team of scientists and teachers from Earth. I and Professor Bhaskaran were thinking that if we can ever face such a crisis….. then will any other planet help us and then will we be able to accept to return to the world without science !!

Science Fiction

ZUNG

'Mom, look, what I brought!' Mayank said as soon as he came from school. He had a stunned puppy in his hands. His mom said, 'Oh! it's so cute! From where did you get it?'

'From Rajan's house. He has more puppies there. Mom, why not we take care of it? No one else would have such a cute and adorable puppy.' Mayank urged his mom.

'Yes, but the computer will check it first.'

'Oh ! Why does this computer come in the middle? Last time I had brought a kitten but it had refused.' Mayanke said with annoyance. His mother explained lovingly, 'Dear, it was ill. If it is healthy then we will take care of it.

Mayank was very happy today. First, dad's permission was obtained and the second, the puppy was successful in the computer test. The computer named it- 'Zung'.

Now Zung started living in the house as a member. Mayank takes care of it in every way. When he came from school, he would first find Zung. Zung also obeys him. Zung would also participate in every activity of Mayank's eating, drinking, sleeping, waking up and sitting. Seeing his closeness with Zung, sometimes Papa would interrupt, but it didn't matter to him.

One day as soon as he came from school, he said to his mother, 'Mom, we are going on a tour with the geography teacher, so she will come home to talk to you in the evening. Please tell her to let Zung take together as well.'

'Okay, I'll see.' Mom said. Mayank started playing with Zung. When the teacher came home in the evening, mom said, 'Mayank is insisting on taking Zung along too.'

'No, it is not possible.' The teacher said, 'We are going on tour for fifteen days. What if all the kids started insisting like this?'

Mom didn't say anything either. Mayank also got busy in his preparation. In the evening, dad came from his

office, Mayank said, 'Dad, I am going on a tour with the teacher. Take care of Zung.' Papa smiled in response.

Early in the morning, the bus came to pick up Mayank. Mayank said again and again, 'Mom, keep an eye on Zung. Bye, bye, mom and dad.'

'Yes, yes, I'll take care. Bye!' Mom said, shaking her hand. By then the bus had gone too far. Mom and dad came in.

After Mayank left, Zung kept searching for him all night. It didn't even take dinner at night. It just kept sobbing all night. Sometimes it used to go to this room and sometimes to that room.

Seeing its restlessness, mom said to dad, 'Ever since Mayank has gone, it keeps on sobbing except food and drink.'

'It will be fine in a day or two,' replied dad while working on the computer. But Zung didn't eat anything the next day either. The whole day it was sitting in a corner. Mom started doing her work. In the evening, as soon as dad came home, mom said in a bewildered voice, 'Zung is not in the house.'

"Since when?" asked dad.

'I don't know, I was doing my work here.' Mom said.

Dad scoured every corner of the house. But Zung was no where. There was no trace of Zung even in the neighbourhood. Dad got the report written in the police station. At this police station, only the lost animals were searched. This police station was dedicated to domestic animals and birds.

It was Sunday. Mom and dad were sad. The news had also come from the police station. Zung had come under a vehicle while running down the road. Mom broke the silence, 'What will you say to Mayank? It will be difficult to handle him.' Then there was a knock on the door. Dad got up and opened the door. Mayank's mama ji was standing in front of him. Mom was very happy to see Mamaji.

Where is Mayank?' Mama ji asked first.

'He has gone on tour on behalf of the school.' Dad said. When mama ji retired from bath. Dad asked, 'Did you get any job or not?'

Yes, I am in Hyderabad. There I am working in a robot company. Some six months have passed.' Then after stopping for a while, Mama ji asked, 'What is the matter brother-in-law? Didi's face has become dry. You are also looking a little sad.'

Dad told the whole incident of the last days. Mom said, 'If the same puppy comes again, So can the matter be resolved?'

'But he won't be able to do like Zung. And then it is not even easy to find a puppy of the same colour.' Dad said.

'Yes indeed.' Mama ji supported.

Mom informed dad and Mama ji that the food was ready.

'I have found the solution.' Mama Ji told dad in the evening. Mom was also sitting there. Dad asked, 'What is the solution?'

"A senior friend of mine is a scientist. He is also working in a higher position in the same company. If we bring a robot dog similar to Zung's gestures!' Mama ji said looking at mom.

'Is it possible?'

'Yes, why not? Bharat Robotics Company Limited also manufactures a wide variety of toys. If we send Zung's picture and gestures, character-related things there, then it is possible that Zung's model will be ready.

'Has the company done this before?' Dad asked in surprise.

'No, but my friend once said that it is possible. Zung's picture will be there. You tell me some important things related to his activities and movements. I will message Professor Bhargava on e-mail.' Mama ji said.

Dad handed over the entire Zung-related report to him. Mama ji said, 'You rest assured. Zung's pattern will be no different from him in the slightest.

It had been thirteen days since Mayank had gone. Mama ji was also gone. The parents were afraid whether a new Zung would come or not. Then there was a knock on the door. Dad opened the door. A man stood in front with Zung in his hands. When dad took Zung, that person also returned without saying anything. By then mom also came.

'Can't believe it, it's a machine. Turn it on.' Mom said quickly. When dad activated new Zung, it went to all the rooms one by one and then started licking dad's feet. Mom's surprise knew no bounds.

Mom said to new Zung, 'From Mayank's room bring his trousers.' Zung brought Mayank's trousers. The new Zung behaved exactly like the old Zung. Within two days, even the parents forgot that Zung was dead.

Fifteen days had passed. Mayank returned from his stay.

'Mom ! It was fun. Where is Zung?' Mayank asked as soon as he came.

'And who's munching on your trousers?' Mom said with a laugh. Mayank said 'hey' and lifted Zung in his lap. 'How naughty it has become, dad!'!' Mayank complained to his father. Dad smiled in response. He was really surprised. Mayank was also deceived. Mayank went to his room with Zung.

'What if Mayank came to know the truth?' Mummy said, expressing doubt.

'No it won't happen. Zung's battery will last for a year. And then his 'switch' is also in a secret place.' Dad assured Mom. Mom peeped into Mayank's room. He was busy playing with Zung. Mom was relieved. Dad went to office.

'Mom, mom, Look what happened to Zung.'

Mayank shouted and came to his mom's room. Mom came out. She quickly went to his room. Mayank said - 'Look, I am feeding it toffee, but it is not eating it. I put three toffees in its mouth but it spews. Mom , why is it doing this?'

'Oh, nothing has happened to it, son. I fed it when you were sleeping.' Mom said. She herself was confused. She didn't even notice the problem.

'Oh ! So you should have told earlier. Zung was also looking at his face and playing with his shirt collar. Mom was even more astonished to see that wonderful mechanical creature. Mayank left Zung and went to his study-room.

When dad came home in the evening, mom said - 'This is a wonderful mechanical creature! It doesn't seem like it's just a device. It does what Mayank says. Its behavior is also similar to 'Zung'. But today a strange thing happened.....'

'What ?'

'Mayank was trying to feed it.' Dad was shocked to hear mom's words - 'Oh! We had not even thought of this. Try to slowly move Mayank away from it. Then called Mayank and said- 'Son,

Zung's digestion is bad. Don't give him things here and there.

"Okay dad." Mayank said.

One day in the evening dad and mom went to visit a friend's house. Mayank stayed at home with Zung. It had been three hours since they left the house.

'We must go now. Mayank will be alone in the house.' Mom said to dad. They were ready to leave when a servant came and said- 'Sir, your phone.....' Dad hung the phone by ear. Mayank's voice came from there - 'Dad, Zung has run away!' Dad was stunned. Zung ran away! Even the machine can run away. When mom heard it, she too was shocked.

They quickly returned home. Mayank cried and said – 'Dad, Jung left the house and ran away.'

"How did it run away?" Dad asked to Mayank.

'When I felt hungry, I thought that Zung must be hungry too. I tried to feed him, but it did not eat. Then I scolded it and said that if mother feeds, you eat and do not eat from me. Run away from here!'

Then Mayank cried and said – 'Dad, Zung ran away.' Dad's mouth was left open in surprise.

Mom said softly- 'Can a mechanical creature feel bad? Mayank went to his room. Papa informed mama ji.

In Hyderabad, Mama ji was talking with his friend Professor Bhargava. When Mama ji was shocked to hear the news, Professor Bhargava asked - 'Why Vinod, why did you get shocked?'

'Zung went away!'

'What ? Professor Bhargava's mouth remained wide open. Mama ji and the professor were also surprised to hear the reason for Zung's escape. They didn't understand how it was possible. Suddenly a thought flashed in Professor Bhargava's mind - 'Oh! Now understood Vinod, Zung's run away is a simple thing.

'How ?'

'Our company only makes robot and toys. Zung was just an imitation of an animal. Only those instructions were 'puffed' into the 'chip' of its computer that pertained to the puppy's temperament and activities. An important characteristic of Zung was obedience. Mayank is sensitive. But what does this mean to the mechanical thing? He scolds and said run away. This scolding was also a command for Zung. Inform your brother-in-law. He must be getting upset.' Professor Bhargava said. Mama ji informed Mayank's dad.

Knowing this, the doubts of the parents were cleared. They both went to Mayank's room. Mom said lovingly - 'Don't be sad son. We will bring a new Zung.

'If it ran away too?' Mayank said with tears. Now who would explain to him that his Zung had not run away? It then.......!

Environment Fiction

The Mother Of Four Sons

This is about that time when we were very young. So young that ghost-vampire, devil-witch etc would keep their permanent camp in our mind. It was very scary to get up at night and go out alone. If the owl used to fly by shouting loudly, then our giggles would have been tied.

Then there were four of us in the troupe – Chunnu, Gopi, Damru and I. Among us, Damru was big and some fearless too. May be that's why he used to dominate us. He used to scold sometimes too. We all went to study in a primary school far from the village. We used to see an old lady's house on the way. The white haired woman used to irrigate the plants. We watched eagerly. But no one went there. Because we were afraid.

The story of old lady is also very strange. She was orphaned in her childhood. Somebody took care of her and she was married to a soldier of the army. In the Indo-Pak war of 1971, her husband was martyred while defending the motherland. Then she came to our village and started living in government land away from our settlement.

When she came, no one knew her. Some people objected to her stay in the village. Whom no one knows, why should he stay in the village. Nobody used to go there. She didn't say anything. She was always doing some work. She used to draw water from the well of our settlement and used to irrigate the plants. No one cared what she was doing.

One day people saw that she was coming towards our settlement carrying a basket full of vegetables on her head. She went from house to house distributing vegetables. At first the women of the village shrugged their nose and eyebrows. Then people's attitude towards her changed. Other women also started visiting her house. Then all our fears also ended.

One day Damru took all three of us to her house. She had made the deserted place green. Many types of trees were swinging in the wind. Various vegetables were planted. Then she came out. She made us all sit and gave guava to eat.

'Grandma, why do you live alone?' One day when Damru asked, She laughed and said- 'Where am I alone. I have four sons and you are all also.

We were surprised. Where are the four sons? We haven't seen anyone. She would laugh and say- 'They take great care of me and I also them'. We all did not understand her riddle. We have never seen her sons. Then how do they take care of grandma? Old grandma is probably joking. She would wake up laughing and start irrigating the plants.

Mother of four sons. But she is always alone. One day Damru asked - 'When will you introduce us to your sons?'

Old grandma would laugh and say - 'Sure you will meet. See, when I die, all my four sons will be with me.

'Why do you say this Amma!' Gopi said softly and grandma laughed. We saw, she was looking at all

of us with great affection. Maybe they liked Gopi's point. Slowly it became our daily routine. We used to spend every evening there. Ate different types of fruits and played different types of games. Slowly more children also started coming.

The day was sad. Chunnu, Gopi and I were ready to go to school. Then Damru came. 'got to know? Grandma is dead.' He said as soon as he came. My father and uncle have gone to see her. Your grandfather has also gone there.

We also went there. Maybe grandma's four sons have also come.

There was a crowd at grandma's house. Grandma was lying at the back of the house. Mouth open and eyes staring at the void. But where are the four sons? Surely grandma must had been joking. But she never lied. Then ? Then our eyes fell on the mango trees. The ever swinging trees stood still today. Oh ! So these four trees are the sons of grandma. 'Look, when I die, I will be with my sons only.' These were her words. We should have understood earlier.

Grandma is no more today, but her four sons still remind of her memory!

ComicStory

The old cucumber

When Jumrati Miya's wife went to her maternal home, she got rest assured and he too became worry-free. He was forgetful in nature. Because of this, his wife often quarreled. When one day the quarrel took a formidable form, she too went to her maternal home with her children. The family members explained – you should not have done this.

Jumrati Miya had a farm. In that he would grow vegetables and eat it throughout the year. He got some cucumber seeds from somewhere and sowed them too.

Several months elapsed. Jumrati Miya did not take any care of his wife. On the other hand, his father-in-law thought - if this happens, then how will the daughter's days be spent, then he decided that he himself will go to convince his son-in-law.

One day when Miya came to visit the field, his eyes fell on the only cucumber left. That plump-fresh cucumber was swinging with pride. 'Oh, I had forgotten it.' He thought in his mind.

He decided to pluck it the next morning.. But that morning did not come for several days. After a few days, that cucumber again came to Jumrati Miya's attention. He immediately went to the farm and saw. The cucumber was fine. I'll pluck it the next morning. With the determination in mind, Jumrati Miya returned home. Then he forgot and decided for the next day. Day by day the cucumber got old. He would remember it throughout the night and forget it in the morning.

One evening his father-in-law came. He was very happy to see his father-in-law. He had forgotten that quarrel. Eating and drinking happened together. His father-in-law also came to know today how much skill he has in cooking. There was no talk about his wife. Father-in-law thought that during the day I will talk to son-in-law. Both the men slept after eating.

In the middle of the night, suddenly Jumrati Miya remembered that cucumber. 'Well done. I will feed it to the father-in-law only.' Thinking of this, he fell asleep. After a while he again remembered that cucumber. 'If I forgot that old cucumber' suddenly a thought flashed in his mind. 'I will not spare that old cucumber!. He started repeating it.

'I will not spare tomorrow! I will not spare tomorrow !! Hearing this, his father-in-law woke up. Jumrati Miyan was murmuring.

'After all, who is he thinking of? About me? It seems, he is thinking so because of a quarrel with my daughter.' As soon as this thought came in his mind, his father-in-law got up silently. He took his bag and started running. Miya felt that there was a thief. He was also no less brave in running. He caught his father-in-law within four furlongs.

'Leave me. I'll never come again The voice came. Miya was shocked to hear father-in-law's voice. 'What happened? why are you so nervous' asked

Miya.

'Oh dear, why don't I panic! Since then you are going to say - 'I will not spare tommorow.' His father-in-law replied. On hearing this, Mian started laughing loudly. Then told them the story of that old cucumber. His father-in-law also started laughing. Both of them came home laughing.

'Miya, don't tell anyone.' His father-in-law said hesitantly.

'I will not say. Now go to sleep.' Jumrati Miya assured him.

Both fell asleep.

In the morning his father-in-law said - 'Just pluck that old.'

'Who old..... for a while, Jumrati Miya said, 'Look, I had forgotten that cucumber again.

Then both of them started laughing together.

Jumrati Miya plucked the cucumber. Both ate it for breakfast. Then Jumrati Miya left for his in-laws' house with his father-in-law.

Old Story

Laddus fight, membranes fall.

Long time ago there lived a thief named Mahavir in a village. He used to do petty thefts in the village but never got caught due to his cunning. Tales of his ingenuity were well known. Even if he was ever caught stealing, but how he would have run away that even the soldiers of the king would not know.

Slowly this matter reached even the king. He announced a reward of two thousand rupees to the person who caught the thief. But no one could catch Mahavir thief.

One night Mahavir entered a house to steal at night. He could not find anything in that house. When he was about to return, he saw a light in a nearby room. He looked inside. An old man was sitting sobbing slowly, and in front of him lay a boy of ten or twelve years old unconscious. The thief went to the old man and asked the reason for his crying.

'What should I say son……' said the old man softly – 'My grandson has been ill for many days and I do not have enough money to get him treated.'

The thief took pity on the old man and the child. He said- 'Baba, I don't have money right now, but I can get it for you.'

'How's that?'

'Baba, I am a thief. The government has placed a reward of two thousand rupees on me. If you get me caught, you can get this reward.' The thief said looking at the young child.

The old man was not ready at first but agreed upon the insistence of the thief. He tied the thief with a rope and took him to the king's court.

'Sir, this thief has been caught stealing in my house. This is the same Mahavir thief on whom you have placed the reward.

‘Well, then you are the same thief who committed big thefts but was never caught. How were you caught today?’

‘Your Majesty, it was probably bad luck today.’ The thief answered, bowing his head.

The old man was given away with a prize. The king looked at the thief. He too had heard tales of the thief’s cunning. He thought of testing his intelligence.

The thief was brought to a strong prison. The king ordered two baskets and laddoos.

‘There are two hundred laddus in these two baskets.’ The king said to the thief – ‘You are imprisoned for a month with these laddoos. On the day you will be free, if one of these laddus is less then you will be hanged. Yes you can get water.

The thief was put in jail.

After a few days, the grandson of that old man also became healthy. He was very sad to hear about the thief. The next day he reached the king’s court.

‘Your Majesty, please free Mahavir.’ The old man said to the king.

'Why? You did say that he had robbed your house.' The king asked in surprise.

'Yes sir, but he is also a generous and kind person.' After that he told the whole story to the king. The king also felt sorrow. It had been a long time since the thief was put in jail.

At the same time the king reached the prison with the old man and others. The guard informed that today the prisoner has not even asked for water.

The king immediately ordered the door to be opened. On opening the door, everyone found the thief in good health. The thief said- 'Maharaj, I could not wake up this morning.'

'Oh, how did you stay safe? You seem to have eaten all the laddus.' The king said angrily.

'Your Majesty, you should count.' said the thief.

When the laddus were counted, no change was found in their number. Everyone was surprised how he survived.

'Maharaj!' Then the thief smiled and said - 'Laddus fight, membranes fall.'

"What do you mean?" asked the king in surprise.

The thief went ahead and put the laddus kept in the first basket to the second, then from the second to the first. After that he ate the membranes of the laddus left in the basket.

'King ! You didn't notice why the size of the laddus became smaller?' The thief said then everyone including the king laughed.

'Mahavir, you are clever and kind-hearted too. I want to put you in the rank of the clown.' The king went ahead and said, hugging the thief. People greeted Mahavir clown with applause.

Mahavira thief became the clown and this proverb also went on - Laddu fought, membranes fell.

Retold Story

Raju And Birds

Summer vacation had started. Raju got some home work to do in these vacation. But he used to play all the day and would not to do his home work. His mother was very annoyed.

One day in the morning, she forcibly asked him to sit down and do home work. But it was difficult for him to concentrate and was not doing it properly.

Sometime later, her mother called him and said that if he has finished his work, he could come and have the breakfast. But he did not reply. He was looking at the birds chirping. He was thinking that these birds have a good life. They do not have to study.

Soon, his sister Sheenu came there to call him and saw him looking at the bird from the window. She saw that he is looking at those birds, very keenly.

As he noticed that Sheenu is standing nearby, he said,-“don’t you think that these birds are enjoying a lot? They do not have to go to school. But what is that in their peaks that they are bringing to this tree.” She said,-“See they are making their home. They are doing hard work to make a place for their children. You should also be hard working like them.”

We would learn from these birds that by dedication and hard work, we can do anything that we want.

Raju realized that she is right in observing the bird while they are making their home. Motivated by the hard work that these birds are doing, he started doing his home work. Their mother was listening to all this from behind. She thanked these birds & her daughter for their contribution.

Retold Story

At Night

Rohan was alone at home and about to go to bed, when he saw a scary shadow figure at his window.

"Who's there" Rohan shouted. Suddenly there was a flash of lightning followed by thundershower.

Rohan saw a lion's face followed by a scary thunderous roar at the window. It looked like the lion from the local circus that had been announced missing on the television news channel. He felt very scared. He ran to his bed and pulled blanket over his head. He started to shout for his parents but there was no reply. Then he remembered they were at a late night party.

party. Rohan peeped out of his blanket but it was too dark to see anything. Then he heard footsteps. They were getting louder and louder. Soon the footsteps died off.

The grand father clock struck 12. Rohan went back to bed and tried to sleep, but couldn't. He felt too frightened. He sat up his mind full of scary thoughts. After some time passed, finally he fell asleep.

Rohan woke up only after eight in the morning and switched on the TV news. He was excited to see the lion was already trapped in the wee hours of the morning by the ring master of the circus. He felt very much relieved after the news.

Later he narrated the whole incident to his parents.

Mom and dad were dumb shocked and decided in future not to leave him alone at home during night.

Retold Story

Farmer And His Sons

There was a farmer at Rampur. He was very hardworking. He has three sons Sohan, Mohan and Godhan. All three were strong and healthy. But they were all lazy. The farmer was sad thinking about his sons and the future of his farmland.

One day, the farmer got a flash of an idea. He called all his sons and said, "Sohan! Mohan! and Godhan! I have hidden a treasure in our farmland. You search and share the treasure among you."

The three sons were overjoyed. They went to the fields and started search.

ing Sohan started from one end. Mohan searched from the other end. And Godhan did so from the centre. They dug each and every inch of the field. But they could not find anything.

The farmer said to his sons, “Dear boys! Now you have tooled and conditioned the field, why not we sow a crop!" Off went the sons to sow the crops.

Days passed. Soon, the crops grew lushly green. The sons were delighted.

The father said, "Sons, this is the real treasure I wanted you to share".

Retold Story

The Ant and the Dove

One hot day, an ant was searching for some water. After walking around for some time, she came to a spring. To reach the spring, she had to climb up a blade of grass. While making her way up, she slipped and fell into the water.

She could have drowned if a dove up a nearby tree had not seen her. Seeing that the ant was in trouble, the dove quickly plucked a leaf and dropped it into the water near the struggling ant. The ant moved towards the leaf and climbed up onto it. Soon, the leaf drifted to dry ground, and the ant jumped out. She was safe at last.

into the water near the struggling ant. The ant moved towards the leaf and climbed up

onto it. Soon, the leaf drifted to dry ground, and the ant jumped out. She was safe at last.

Just at that time, a hunter nearby was about to throw his net over the dove, hoping to trap it.

Guessing what he was about to do, the ant quickly bit him on the heel. Feeling the pain, the hunter dropped his net. The dove was quick to fly away to safety.

www.ingramcontent.com/pod-product-compliance
Lightning Source LLC
La Vergne TN
LVHW020525160826
845677LV00015B/3914

* 9 7 9 8 4 1 3 8 5 6 2 5 3 *